# IT'S ME

Yehuda Atlas

# IT'S ME

Translated by Roslyn Lacks
Illustrations by Danny Kerman

Adama Books
New York

© 1985 by Yehuda Atlas and Adama books

Library of Congress Cataloging in Publication Data

Atlas, Yehuda, 1937-
  It's me

  Translation of: Veha-yeled ha-zeh hu ani
  Summary: A boy experiences typical problems such as being hit by a
bully, breaking something, and worrying about losing his mother in a
crowd.
  1. Children's stories, Hebrew. [1. Stories in rhyme] I. Title.
PZ8.3.A9213It 1985 [E] 85-1239

ISBN 0-915361-20-5

Adama Books, 306 West 38 Street, New York, N.Y. 10018
Printed in Israel

Just an empty can
someone threw away,
'tho I pass it by
when I'm on my way,
something stops me short
and makes me look back,
turn on my heels
and give it a whack.

1

I knew
I was really grown
the day
I tied my shoelaces
all on my own.

Just when they're watching TV
and I'm ready for bed,
the hardest questions
pop into my head.
It might make them angry,
but I really can't wait
'cause "later"
is always too late.

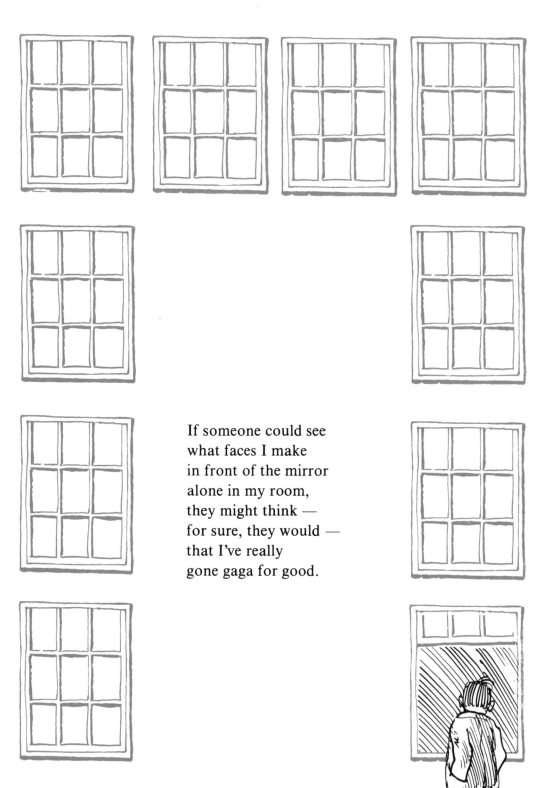

If someone could see
what faces I make
in front of the mirror
alone in my room,
they might think —
for sure, they would —
that I've really
gone gaga for good.

I never
know why
they make me wear boots
and say,
"Keep dry!"

5

Maybe it's really insulting
and hard for them to believe,
but whenever
I'm kissed
on the face
I wipe it off with my sleeve.

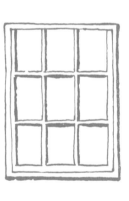

In a street full of people,
what scares me most
is that mommy will disappear
and I'll be lost.

A fancy lady came one day
wearing smells from far away.
She put her pocket book
aside;
didn't say
if there was
or wasn't
a present
inside.

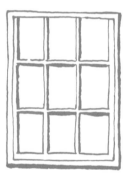

She talked and talked
between sips of tea,
then suddenly stopped
and turned to me.
"Honey," she said, crossing her knees,
"Would you get my bag, please?"

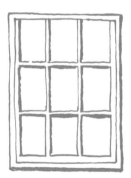

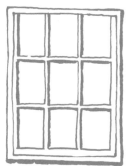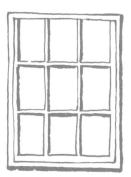

I touched it
hush-hush,
clutched it
without a blush.
Gee, I could swear
something was there!
Soft rustling and crinkling
gave me the inkling.
Maybe that's why
when I delivered it,
my hand shivered a bit.

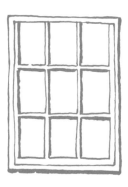

She kissed me and said
I was sweet as a chocolate snack,
reached in her purse and took out
her lighter and cigarette pack.
"Now sweetie," she turned to say,
"Please get the ashtray."

The most terrific
fun of all
is when my uncle
comes to call.

He lifts me, throws me
like a ball
up as high
as he is tall.

"Take it easy,"
Dad would tell us,
but I really
think he's jealous.

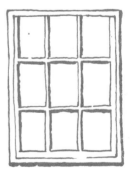

When the scary thing
crawled into my room,
the night I was sick,
I called daddy
to come quick —
and he came
when he heard me shout;
but the moment he walked in,
the thing walked out.

If I were
the child of the owner
of the candy store
around the corner,
I would eat chocolates
all the time
and never ever
pay a dime.

When I tell you something,
and you say,
"That's nice, I see..."
I can tell
you're not
listening
to me.

When mom is sleeping
and I need to tell her
something,
I try to wake her
softly, softly
so she won't
wake up.

When you say,
"Promise?"
I say, "You bet!"
Can I help it
if later
I seem to forget?

15

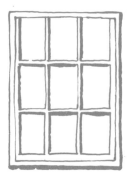

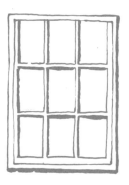

When you say,
"Careful, don't break!"
I try to hold on,
but my hands start to shake.
It feels like the first time,
but it's happened before —
whatever I'm holding
ends up on the floor.

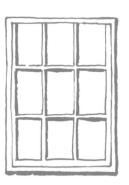

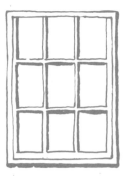

16

What I want,
what I'm dying to get
is a puppy,
my very own pet.

If I can't have that,
I'd like mother
to get me at least
a sister or brother.

17

Even if I were fat as a hippo
and couldn't get through the door,
grandma would still keep saying,
"Why don't you eat some more?"

Walking in the garden
after light summer showers,
I found deep puddles
on paths between flowers.

I made a bridge over one
with a stick that just fit;
later, when I watched,
an ant crossed over it.

Just when we're in a hurry,
both of us,
we have many
important things to discuss.
But when there's lots of time
while taking a walk,
and I say,
"Dad, let's talk,"
suddenly
we run out of words
and clump along
like two dodo birds.

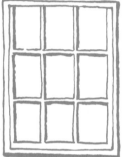

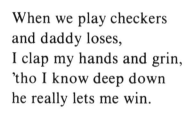

When we play checkers
and daddy loses,
I clap my hands and grin,
'tho I know deep down
he really lets me win.

21

Every time the phone rings,
I run to pick it up.
The call won't be for me
I know,
but I just love
to say hello.

22

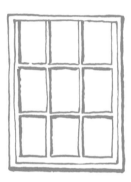

If you want to make me
go to bed before you do
then turn off the TV
so you'll miss it too.

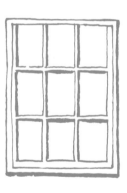

Putting my hand
in my coat pocket
the first day of frost,
and finding the penknife
I thought
I had lost.

If I could make a wish
like they do in a fairy tale,
I'd ask to grow
a short fluffy tail.
What for?
I'm not sure.
Maybe just
to go outside
and have it wag
from side to side.

25

Daddy makes pickles
at home,
but he's always hurt to see
that the ones I like much more
are those we buy at the store.

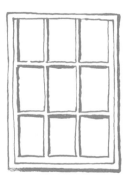

When mommy helps me
on with my sweater,
she'd like me to hold on
to my shirt cuff better,
but I lose my grip,
the sleeve starts to slip
and bunches
up to my shoulder.
Then when mommy slides
her fingers inside
to smooth it down straight,
it feels really great!

If a child runs away
after hitting me from behind,
I plan such terrible revenge
he's lucky it slips my mind.

28

The apple
that fell on the floor
I'd already
eaten in part,
but the one
mommy gave me instead,
I have
to begin from the start.

My winter blanket cover
has a missing piece
on the upper side —
just enough for me
to crawl and dig myself
inside.

When mommy peels an orange,
it comes out whole and dry;
but when I try to do it,
it turns into mush pie.

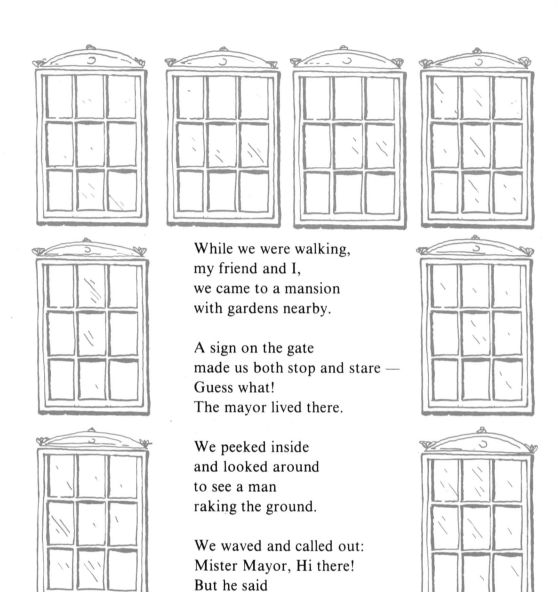

While we were walking,
my friend and I,
we came to a mansion
with gardens nearby.

A sign on the gate
made us both stop and stare —
Guess what!
The mayor lived there.

We peeked inside
and looked around
to see a man
raking the ground.

We waved and called out:
Mister Mayor, Hi there!
But he said
he's only the gardener.

Every day
I call my father
at work
asking
if he's going to bring me
something.
Maybe it's not very nice
to ask for gifts, yet
if I don't remind him,
he's sure to forget.

More than strong kids
who know how to fight,
I'm scared of cry babies
who hit out of fright.

When I want to be cuddled
and daddy sits huddled
over the paper in his armchair,
I inch up to stand
just under his hand,
moving my head here and there,
'til before he knows it,
he's stroking my hair.

When I turn on the faucet
and cold water drips,
I wash my hands, but
only the fingertips.

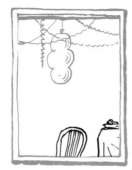

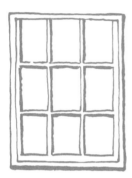

The day of my birthday
I waited for so long,
I burst into tears
'cause everything went wrong.

It always happens:
what I hope for most
turns out worst.

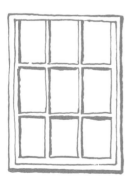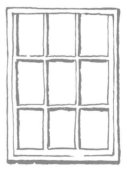

When I get salad,
I want soup.
When I get soup,
I want a hamburger.
When I get a hamburger,
I want French fries.
But when I get chocolate,
I want chocolate.

Far from home,
I don't know why —
I got hit by a bully
and started to cry.

On the way home
it stopped. But when
I saw mommy —
it started again.

39

The potato
we put in the campfire —
nobody
ate it at all;
by the time
we ran back to get it,
it had turned
into smoldering coal.

40

When a friend
comes to play
and picks a toy
from my shelf,
it's always
the one
I want most
myself.

Even when I'm a grandfather,
white hair all over my head,
I'll ask daddy
to tell me a story
after I'm tucked into bed.

Unwrapping
my birthday gifts,
I hope I won't find
new shirts or socks
or things of that kind.

You can't expect me
to stand up and cheer
over stuff I get anyway
all through the year.

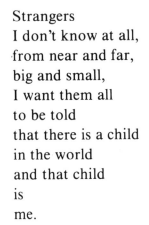

Strangers
I don't know at all,
from near and far,
big and small,
I want them all
to be told
that there is a child
in the world
and that child
is
me.

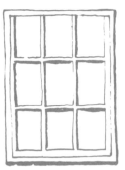